For my lovely mum, who had
an artist's eyes – F.T.

For my dad, who lent me his
brushes – C.M.

Brimming with creative inspiration, how-to
projects, and useful information to enrich your
everyday life, quarto.com is a favourite destination
for those pursuing their interests and passions.

Inspiring | Educating | Creating | Entertaining

An Artist's Eyes © 2022 Quarto Publishing Plc.
Text © 2022 Frances Tosdevin
Illustration © 2022 Clémence Monnet
First published in 2022 by First Editions, an initiative
of Frances Lincoln Children's Books,
an imprint of The Quarto Group,
The Old Brewery, 6 Blundell Street,
London N7 9BH, United Kingdom.
T (0)20 7700 6700 F (0)20 7700 8066 www.Quarto.com

A catalogue record for this book is available from the British
Library.

ISBN 978-0-7112-6483-0
eISBN 978-0-7112-6484-7

Illustrated in gouache, pencil, Indian ink and collage
Set in Bellota

Published by Katie Cotton & Peter Marley
Commissioned and edited by Lucy Brownridge
Designed by Zoë Tucker
Production by Dawn Cameron

Printed in Guangdong, China TT012022
9 8 7 6 5 4 3 2 1

MIX
Paper from
responsible sources
FSC® C016973

An Artist's Eyes

Frances Tosdevin
& Clémence Monnet

Look at **Mo's** eyes.

Now look at **Jo's** eyes.
They look the same.
Friendly,
oval-shaped
and smiley.

But Mo's eyes
are **different** . . .

. . . for Mo has an **artist's eyes**.

"Let's look for **colours**," said Mo.
"Over there," said Jo. "The sea's so **blue!**"

"It's beautiful," said Mo.
"I see a dazzling **duck-egg blue**, a swirl of
peacocks and the inky, **indigo** of evening.
Can you see those colours in the sea, Jo?"

"No. . ." said Jo. "I can't. But look, Mo . . .

" . . . that forest is **green**."

"Gorgeous!" said Mo. "When I look,
I see a shiny **apple-green**; the **lime** of
gooseberries and the springy **zinginess** of **moss**.
See how the shadows make the greens darker?"

"Not like you
can," said Jo.

As they walked, Jo tried with all
his might to see what Mo saw.
"Look, Mo — the flowers in that field . . .

"... are **bright yellow.**"

"So many shades," said Mo. "Notice how **light** changes the colour. I see the **mellow yellow** of **melons** and the pale **pastel** of **primroses**. Can you see them, Jo?"

"**No,**" sighed Jo. "I can't see what you see. It's not fair!"

Then Jo's eyes drooped shut . . .

. . . and he saw only **BLACK**.

"Take your time," said Mo. "When you're
ready, look around and tell me what you see.
Whatever comes into your head."

Jo blinked his eyes open.

"I see the sea. But not your duck and peacock colours. Just blue, with **sparkly** bits."

"How wonderful," said Mo. "And the field of flowers? What catches your eye?"
"They're sort of **swirly** to me," said Jo.
"Not primrosey, like you saw."

"You're doing really well!" said Mo, squeezing Jo's hand. "Now, what about the forest. What do you see there?"

"Just pointy patterns
in the green," sighed Jo,
kicking the ground.

"But **look** over there, Mo. . .

". . . those leaves
are **really red.**"

"You're right!" said Mo.
"There's yellow-red, orange-red,
and purple-red. Can you see
all those shades?"

"No!" said Jo.
He felt his face flush
with failure. "I'll **never**
see like an artist."

Jo stamped his foot so hard
that leaves fluttered all around.
Red thoughts raged through his head.
"Just **trust** your own eyes, Jo," said
Mo. "See what they show you."

Jo shrugged. He took a deep breath.
Then he tried with all his SIGHT . . .

It was a bit tricky at first.
Where Mo saw **plump**, purple
plums, with flecks of chocolate
and night-time,

Jo saw **ovals**
in **mauve** rows.

Where Mo saw **pinky-lilac** pigeons with slatey backs, Jo marvelled at **feathery fans** in flight.

Where Mo saw every shade of autumn on the forest floor,

Jo gasped at the footprints of tiny, **colourful dinosaurs!**

Now he was really **seeing**.

As they headed home, Jo pointed out
swirly circles of sunshine, **thin triangles**
of trees and **sparkly squiggles** on the sea.

Jo showed Mo lots of exciting sights. Some things Mo could see — but some she couldn't. "You're doing really well," said Jo, squeezing Mo's hand.

As the sun slipped away, the stars washed
everything with shadowy, silvery light.
Both Mo and Jo saw every speck.
But they saw it all quite
differently.

Snuggling at home, Mo's eyes
and Jo's eyes look the same.
Friendly, oval-shaped
and sleepy . . .

. . . two pairs of artists' eyes,
ready for unique dreams.